Daniel Gets His Hair Cut

Adapted by Jill Cozza-Turner
Based on the screenplay "Daniel's First Haircut"
written by Jill Cozza-Turner & Holly Walker
Poses and layouts by Jason Fruchter

Simon Spotlight
New York   London   Toronto   Sydney   New Delhi

SIMON SPOTLIGHT
An imprint of Simon & Schuster Children's Publishing Division
1230 Avenue of the Americas, New York, New York 10020
This Simon Spotlight paperback edition May 2019
© 2019 The Fred Rogers Company
SIMON SPOTLIGHT and colophon are registered trademarks of Simon & Schuster, Inc.
For information about special discounts for bulk purchases, please contact Simon & Schuster
Special Sales at 1-866-506-1949 or business@simonandschuster.com.
Manufactured in the United States of America 0423 LAK
10 9 8 7 6 5
ISBN 978-1-5344-4327-3
ISBN 978-1-5344-4328-0 (eBook)

It was a beautiful day in the neighborhood! Daniel was drawing some funny faces, but his hair kept falling into his eyes.

"Grr. Stay up there, hair!" said Daniel.

"Hmmm . . . ," said Dad Tiger. "Your hair has grown longer."

Daniel was confused. He hadn't felt his hair grow!
"Growing happens even when you don't feel it," said Dad Tiger.
Daniel didn't like his hair in his eyes.
"Then that means it's time for your first haircut," said Dad Tiger.

Daniel had never had a haircut before.
Dad sang, *"When we do something new, let's talk about what we'll do!"*
"Let's talk about your haircut," said Dad.
"What's a haircut like?" asked Daniel.

Dad explained that when you get a haircut, a hairdresser or barber gently holds your hair and then cuts the ends with scissors.

"Hey . . . ," said Daniel. "That looks good!"

"Then let's go get your hair cut!" said Dad.

They headed out to the salon. Daniel was excited to get his hair cut but a little nervous too. Who would cut his hair?

Daniel was so happy to see . . . Nana Platypus! She was cutting Prince Tuesday's hair!

"I didn't know you cut hair!" said Daniel.

"I sure do!" said Nana.

Snip-snip-snip! Nana used her special scissors to cut Prince Tuesday's hair.

"Does your haircut . . . hurt, Prince Tuesday?" asked Daniel.

Prince Tuesday told Daniel that it doesn't hurt at all!

Nana's blow-dryer made a whirring noise as she dried Prince Tuesday's hair. Soon, Prince Tuesday's haircut was over and his hair was a little shorter.

"It looks grr-ific!" said Daniel.

"Thanks, Little D," said Prince Tuesday. "See you later!"

After Prince Tuesday left, Miss Elaina and Lady Elaine entered the salon.

Miss Elaina was excited. Nana Platypus was going to braid her hair today!

"Who wants to go first?" asked Nana.
Daniel wasn't ready for his haircut yet. Miss Elaina couldn't wait for her braids, so she got into the special chair first.

♪ ♪ "When we do something ♪ ♪
new, let's talk about what we'll
do!" Nana sang.
    Nana told Miss Elaina what
she was going to do. "I'm going
to lift my chair up-up-up. . . ."

Next Nana put a cape on
Miss Elaina. Nana told her that
the cape would keep her clothes
clean and dry while she styled
her hair.
    Miss Elaina felt like a
superhero with a backward
cape!

"Now it's time to sit still," said Nana.
Miss Elaina sat very still. Nana Platypus brushed out her hair before she started braiding it.

Nana braided Miss Elaina's hair and put colorful barrettes at the bottom of each one. The barrettes made a *clickety-clack* sound when they bounced together!

Snip-snip-snip! Whir-whir-whir! Clickety-clack! There are so many sounds at the hair salon!

Daniel imagined what getting a haircut would be like if everything in the hair salon made music!

Brush, brush—they'll brush your hair!
Spray, spray—everywhere!
Let's wash, wash—wash your hair!
Snip, snip! You're almost there!
When your hair gets too long on top,
let's head down to the barbershop!

"All done!" said Nana Platypus.
"Look at my boomerific braids!" said Miss Elaina. "I love them!"
Daniel liked them too!

"Now it's time for your haircut, Daniel," said Nana Platypus. But Daniel didn't know if he was ready for his haircut.

Nana sang, *"When we do something new, let's talk about what we'll do!"*

"Come sit in my chair!" said Nana.

Nana told Daniel what she was going to do. "First you'll go up-up-up!"

"Wheeee!" said Daniel.

Then she put a cape on Daniel just as she had done on Miss Elaina.

"Now I'll spray your hair with water," said Nana.

"What is that for?" wondered Daniel.

"Sometimes I spray water on hair so it's easier to cut," said Nana.

Spray-spray-spray! It felt cool and a little wet!

Daniel was ready for Nana to cut his hair.
"Okay," said Nana. "Now it's time for you to sit still."
Daniel sat as still as he could. Nana's scissors went *snip-snip-snip*.
"Hey . . . that doesn't hurt at all!" said Daniel.

"All done!" said Nana.
Daniel's hair wasn't in his eyes anymore!
"I like my new haircut! Thank you, Nana," said Daniel.
"You're very welcome," she replied.
Everyone liked Daniel's new haircut. Dad Tiger even took a picture!

Daniel was a little nervous about his first haircut, but when he talked about what he'd do, he felt better—and you can too, neighbor. Ugga Mugga!